I am sure you all know me!
I'm the famous movie star Youpala.
People wave to me and hug me in the street.
I get dozens of letters from my fans every day.
But I bet you don't know how I got to be
an actress in the first place.

So listen to this!
My first movie was called:

Queen of the Jungle

KINGFISHER
Larousse Kingfisher Chambers Inc.
95 Madison Avenue
New York, New York 10016

First American edition 1995
2 4 6 8 10 9 7 5 3 1

Copyright © Éditions Nathan (Paris-France) 1991
English translation copyright © Larousse plc 1995

LIBRARY OF CONGRESS CATALOGING-IN-PUBLICATION DATA
Youpala.
Youpala, queen of the jungle / written by Youpala;
illustrated by Zaü.—1st American ed.
p. cm.
Summary: Now a famous movie star, Youpala recalls how
she came to make her first film.
[1. Jungles–Fiction. 2. Motion pictures–Production and direction–Fiction.]
I. Zaü, ill. II. Title.
PZ7.Y8957Yo 1995
[Fic]–dc20 94-48719 CIP AC

ISBN 1-85697-625-4

YOUPALA
QUEEN OF THE JUNGLE

Written by Youpala
English text by Anthea Bell
Illustrated by Zaü

Kingfisher

NEW YORK

This is the story of a little girl called Youpala. I am Youpala. Everyone in my village calls me Youpala Impalapa, which means *the little girl who asks thousands of questions*, because I ask questions all the time.

I love my village.

I can spend whole days watching the women cooking flat cakes of bread or drying their laundry on stones steaming in the sun.

I like talking to old Yambo, who sells bright beads to wear on feast days.

I like going to market to buy pineapples and loquats, okra and breadfruit.

I like breathing in the smell of the fruits and vegetables and listening to the old women singing as they sell their wares.

I like bathing in the river and playing with my friends Bila and Pimkoko, who herd goats in the tall grass of the savanna.

I like listening to the stories told by Timpokeke, the village witch doctor, and seeing the hunters go off in the evening to catch antelopes for our food.

But what I like best of all is going out in secret when night falls. I like to leave my home and sit at the edge of the jungle. There I can hear the song of the wind in the trees, the cries of the monkeys squabbling, and the long, deep roars of lions out hunting.

And I dream . . .

I dream of being queen of the jungle some day—
Queen Youpala Impalapa, the little girl who asks
thousands of questions!
I dream . . .

. . . This time I went off into the jungle all alone.
I waited for it to be afternoon, when everyone in
the village lies down for a nap, and the skinny cows
sleep in the shade of the old well. Then I set out.

I walked through the forest. I walked and walked.

I saw monkeys swinging from creeper to creeper.
I heard parrots squawking in the trees.

All of a sudden I heard a loud rustling in the
branches. What could it be? I was scared.

hen I saw two bright eyes looking at me, two bright eyes devouring me greedily. A lion! I wanted to run away and hide. The lion climbed a tree and disappeared.

"My goodness me!" I said to myself. "I never knew lions could climb trees!"

But I thought nothing of it, and decided that the lion was afraid of me.

Just then I heard a voice calling:
"*Queen of the Jungle!* Take one!"
And there was a clacking sound. How strange!

But I went on. I walked through the jungle—
I walked and walked and walked.

All of a sudden I heard a funny clicking noise.
Click, click, clickety- click, it went. Walking toward
the sound, I saw a crocodile sitting up on its hind
legs, knitting a sweater.

"My goodness me!" I said to myself. "I never
knew crocodiles could knit!"

But I thought nothing of it, and decided the
crocodile was knitting the sweater for me.

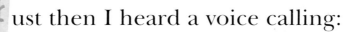ust then I heard a voice calling:
"*Queen of the Jungle!* Take two!"
And I heard that strange clacking sound again.
But I didn't stop—I walked through the jungle.
I walked and walked and walked.

All of a sudden I heard the clinking of china.
It sounded like teacups clinking. Then I saw a
giraffe sitting at a table, crooking its little finger
as it drank a cup of tea.

"Would you like some tea?" the giraffe asked me.

"My goodness me!" I said to myself. "I never
knew giraffes drank tea!"

But I thought nothing of it, and decided the giraffe was simply being polite.

Just then I heard a loud voice saying:

"Good gracious me, little girl, what on earth are you doing here?"

And I saw a man with a loudspeaker come out of the bushes. He looked very cross.

Then I saw the lion come down from the tree,
and I saw the crocodile put its knitting away,
and I saw the giraffe finish its cup of tea.
The man came up to me and said,
"Can't you see we're making a movie? Now we'll
have to begin all over again, just because of you!"

I didn't understand a word he said. I had no idea what a movie was. Luckily, a man with a camera whispered something to the first man, who was the director.

"Wait a moment," he said. "Don't be cross with her! I've just been watching the takes. This little girl is very good! Maybe we could hire her to play the lead?"

So that is how I, Youpala Impalapa, got to be a movie star.

And the movie is called *Queen of the Jungle.*

The village held a big party to celebrate. All the movie people were invited, and all the animals, too. Everybody danced around the fire and sang.

Timpokeke the witch doctor told stories, Bila and Pimkoko played their pipes, and as for me, Youpala Impalapa, I asked thousands of questions.

Meanwhile, out in the jungle, the monkeys were squabbling, the parrots were squawking, and the lions were roaring loud and long as they went hunting.